*The Traveling Yellow Purse*

# THE TRAVELING YELLOW PURSE

Glenda Jensen

ReadersMagnet, LLC

## Shout Outs

I was told by a group of students that dedications are no longer used. I was told if you wanted to just say, "Hey" or "Hello" to someone, just give them a 'shout out'. Below is a list of those to whom I wish to give a "Shout Out".

**1. Delbert Roland Binkley Jr.**

*My husband in Heaven who encouraged me to begin writing upon my retirement*

**2. My Kids**

*Michael Glen Hill*

*Kristina Leigh Hill Canales*

*Desire'e Lynn Dulong Stone*

**3. My Grandkids**

*Kayla Michelle Grant*

*Savanna Leigh Grant*

*Ruby Jean Stone*

*Megan Briar Hill*

*Payton Michelle Hill*

*Travis Wesley Stone*

**4. My Parents**

*Glenroy Richard Jensen*

*Barbara Lolita Robbins Jensen*

# THE TRAVELING YELLOW PURSE

Glenda Jensen

ReadersMagnet, LLC

## Shout Outs

I was told by a group of students that dedications are no longer used. I was told if you wanted to just say, "Hey" or "Hello" to someone, just give them a 'shout out'. Below is a list of those to whom I wish to give a "Shout Out".

**1. Delbert Roland Binkley Jr.**

*My husband in Heaven who encouraged me to begin writing upon my retirement*

**2. My Kids**

*Michael Glen Hill*

*Kristina Leigh Hill Canales*

*Desire'e Lynn Dulong Stone*

**3. My Grandkids**

*Kayla Michelle Grant*

*Savanna Leigh Grant*

*Ruby Jean Stone*

*Megan Briar Hill*

*Payton Michelle Hill*

*Travis Wesley Stone*

**4. My Parents**

*Glenroy Richard Jensen*

*Barbara Lolita Robbins Jensen*

# THE TRAVELING YELLOW PURSE

## FOREWORD

First of all, I want to happily share with my readers that I have finally found that perfect Yellow purse to be added to the already family of purses neatly nestled within my closet. Once I got it home and after carefully inspecting my new purchase, I began to wonder just how my purse began its journey.

Normally, I write stories from the perspective of the third person; however, I wanted to explore something different along with a little humor mixed up with emotion and drama. This story will be written in first person from the point of view of my yellow purse.

Now if you are totally and completely confused by now, read on and the mystery will soon begin to unravel.

*The Traveling Yellow Purse.*
Copyright © 2022 by Glenda Jensen.

Published in the United States of America.

ISBN  Paperback:    978-1-958030-00-4
ISBN  eBook:        978-1-958030-01-1

All rights reserved. No part of this publication may be reproduced, stored in a retrieval system or transmitted in any way by any means, electronic, mechanical, photocopy, recording or otherwise without the prior permission of the author except as provided by USA copyright law.

The opinions expressed by the author are not necessarily those of ReadersMagnet, LLC.

ReadersMagnet, LLC
10620 Treena Street, Suite 230 | San Diego, California, 92131 USA
1.619. 354. 2643 | www.readersmagnet.com

Book design copyright © 2022 by ReadersMagnet, LLC. All rights reserved.

*Cover design by Kent Gabutin*
*Interior design by Dorothy Lee*

# Table of Contents

*Foreword* ............................................................................... v

**Chapter One:** The Journey Begins ............................................... 1
**Chapter Two:** America ................................................................. 5
**Chapter Three:** Walmart: Dallas, Texas ........................................ 8
**Chapter Four:** The Runaway ....................................................... 12
**Chapter Five:** The Purse Snatcher ............................................... 16
**Chapter Six:** Homeless Hannah ................................................. 20
**Chapter Seven:** Thrift Store Saga ................................................ 24
**Chapter Eight:** Lady Gretchen .................................................... 28
**Chapter Nine:** The Estate Sale .................................................... 34
**Chapter Ten:** The Final Destination ........................................... 38

*Epilogue* ................................................................................ 41
*About The Author* ................................................................ 42

# CHAPTER ONE
## *THE JOURNEY BEGINS*

On September 12, 2002, I was not born, but made. Yes, that's right, "made." You see, my friends, I am a purse, not just any purse but a special yellow purse.

My very existence began with an idea in a company located in Indonesia. I know this because there is a tag attached to my lining stating just that. Now I know you don't want to hear about how the idea was put to paper and all that other business-type stuff. So, I'm just gonna jump right into my story.

When I first came into existence, I realized that I was on a conveyor belt while travelling through an assembly line. After my lining was sewn inside, the outer edges were attached together. Then came my handles and a shoulder strap. Finally, zippers, clasps, and decorations were added. At last, I was complete.

My next stop was the packing department. Talk about chaos! There were people everywhere working at what seemed a sonic speed. Not to mention boxes, boxes, and yet more boxes. Sheesh! I found myself being anxious and excited, yet calm. Who was I kidding? I had no unearthly idea where I was going. So I began pondering on this. Was I going to England? Now that would be a kick! I could be the newest member of Queen Elizabeth's purse collection or perhaps Princess Kate's purse family. Wow! Or, was I headed off to Spain or Italy? Just when I had exhausted all guesses, my curiosity had been founded. I was travelling to America! Yes, folks, the good ole US of A. I was so pleased with this and doubly excited. I was also pleased to know that I would be travelling among friends, fellow purses. I love this trip already.

As I was being packed in a large brown cardboard box, I couldn't help but notice the different purses which were going with me. There were brown ones, red ones, black and white ones. There was even a green one and an orange one! There were large purses and small ones, too. By the way, I'm somewhere in the middle. Plus, I do believe that I am the only yellow purse. Imagine that!

Off I go into the wild blue yonder. No, I'm not talking about the sky. We were travelling by cargo ship. The boxes were loaded onto what looked like a railroad car. Then we were hoisted up onto the ship. This ship was so big; it would take 1,000s of us purses to fill it up. But of course, there were not just purses aboard. I do believe there were dresses, hats, and other attire. Anyway off we go. It seemed like I felt every wave; I was jostled against my fellow purses. Were there any complaints? Of course not! Purses don't talk! That would be weird on the borderline of scary. We just have thoughts, but no one knows that.

I remember one time when we encountered a storm. I was worried that we were going to get wet, but I remembered that we were packed in plastic for that very reason. The ship tossed and tossed, up and down. It was a good thing that I was not human for I would probably be seasick at about this time. Hmmmm, I wonder if anyone was. Finally, the ship calmed down, and all was good again.

Every once in a while someone would come into the cargo area and check on us. Boxes were tapped on and kicked just to be sure there wasn't any water damage, and all was good. When the men were on breaks, they would come join us for a friendly game of cards. I could not tell you the specific game, but I knew they were having a good time. Sometimes one of them would get mad and walk away while the others would be laughing. They spoke in a language which I could not understand. After all, I can only understand the language of "Purse." Is there a language? I really don't know. All I do know is that we can sense what each other is thinking and feeling. Kind of scary, huh? Nah, not really. No human knows we can do this, and no one will know, not even someone who can read minds. All they would get is a blank. So, no worries, my friends.

What seemed like months were only a few days, seven to be exact. After all, there are no restaurants, gas stations, or anything else to stop at here in the middle of the ocean. We just kept skipping over the waves, day in and day out – the same ole thing every day. Even though this activity may have come across to be boring, my enthusiasm was ever present.

It seemed like a k-zillion (is this a number?) years before land was sighted on the horizon. Was it the United States, Nova Scotia, or maybe Canada?

*The Traveling Yellow Purse*

I thought I heard someone shout "Statue of Liberty" or something like that. How was I to know? I was in a cardboard box. The information that we were finally in America, better yet New York, came to me when we were being loaded off the ship. Land, at last! If I had had lips, I would have literally kissed the ground!

# CHAPTER TWO
## *AMERICA*

America! Here at last! Just like in Indonesia, there were people scuttling around just like roaches when the lights come on. Yes, I have encountered a few of these creatures while on the ship. Thank goodness for the plastic which I was wrapped in.

Now that I was on solid ground again, I kept wondering what was going to happen to me next. Suddenly, we were being lifted up in the air as if by magic. I soon found out that it was a forklift used by humans to aid in lifting heavy objects. After we were lifted up, we began moving again. This time the movement simulated a floating cloud. Yes, I do know what clouds are. You see, purses are extremely knowledgeable. We know a lot of things, but yet humans do not know that about us. (Just another one of our little secrets.)

We finally reached our destination. We were in a large room among other boxes. What seemed like hours later, our box was suddenly opened. Looming above were two humans dressed in uniforms – custom relations officers. They also had a fairly large sized dog with them which was sniffing around our box. Not only was he sniffing outside but also inside. What an invasion! Can't a purse get any privacy! I wasn't sure what they were looking for at the time. But all they found were a few dead roaches and a bunch of plastic-wrapped purses. I learned later from purse, which had been in America for a while, that these people were looking for drugs. Imagine that! In a purse! Well I never! But yet that is another story all together.

After we were checked out, the two officers reclosed and taped our box then slapped a sticker on it suggesting that we passed the customs check point.

Again with the forklift, we were lifted up and taken to yet another loading dock. The only difference was that this one would seal our fate. Again my enthusiasm came to the surface again, and my curiosity kicked in high gear. I pondered the question (I pondered lots of questions during this journey), "Where was I going? Was I going to stay here in New York or was I headed to California or even Florida?" I was completely clueless. But yet again I was to experience the waiting game.

Two weeks had passed, and we were still in the cardboard box. I was beginning to think that we would be here forever. As Winnie the Pooh would say, "Oh bother." (Note: If you don't know who Winnie is, I feel sorry for you.) Because you see I do know who this little bear is. In the world of purses, word travels fast like the wind through the trees of a forest. What seemed like an eternity, we were lifted up once more by a forklift. Boy, these humans sure use this contraption a lot. This time we were put into a truck, an eighteen wheeler to be exact. What excitement! This means were headed to our final place and to finally be let out of the box. Happiness was in the air!

Another question I pondered, "Where were we headed?" Then it hit me like a ton of bricks. Texas! Yes, my friends, we were on our way to the lone star state. Yee haw! I heard that cowboys said this quite a bit. I wonder if cowgirls carry purses. But I guess so, because that's where we were headed. But where in Texas: Austin, Houston, or San Antonio? The thoughts in the truck told me that we were making tracks to the Big D, Dallas.

So Dallas, Texas, get ready for the thrill of your life. I am not sure just how long the trip would take from New York to Dallas, but it seemed to last just as long as the trip on the ocean only this time we made several stops, restaurants, gas stations, road side parks, and a couple of motels a time or two. Anyway it seemed to be a very long time. I found out later that it would take at least 1,000 miles. Wow!

My next question which I began to ponder was, "What store were we going to?" Were we going to Macys, Sears, Nordstrom, or even Lord and Taylor? A couple of these stores are really exclusive, and shoppers have to have lots of money to shop there. Hmmmmm. Now that would be interesting. I began to dream of being in someone's closet who was a VIP (Very Important Person) such as the mayor's wife or the daughter of an attorney. These dreams soon came to an abrupt halt when the truck finally stopped.

# CHAPTER THREE
# *WALMART: DALLAS, TEXAS*

We had arrived. As we were being unloaded, it was discovered that the store we were assigned to was a Walmart. Of all places! Really? Nothing against Walmart, but I was really hoping on one of those fancy stores. Oh well. Lots of people shop Walmart. I had hoped that someone nice would purchase me, and I would find my permanent home.

So off we went, my fellow purses and I, to be put on display where accessories were usually located, somewhere near the middle of the store. Luckily, I was on top of the heap along with my best friends, the green purse and the orange one. We were the special purses because we were different from the rest, in color and style, that is. Then came the white purses. After they were unpacked, the red ones were next. Last but not least came the black and brown ones. On a good note, those horrible plastic wraps came off. It felt so good not to have my handles so scrunched up. It also felt good to feel clean air again.

We each had our own separate hook, so we could look proud, clean, and new. I could not wait to find out just were I would find my new permanent home. At this time, I had no clue that I would be thrown into an adventure of which I would remember for the rest of my existence.

Day in and day out, week in and week out, nobody would purchase me. Boo hoo! This was a sad time for me because I was beginning to think that no one would want to buy a special yellow purse. Just as I thought all hope was lost, it got worse.

Christmas time was just around the corner, and all was a bustle in the store. It had been approximately six months since I began my journey. I really had no way keeping time or what month it was. After all I was either on an assembly line, in a cardboard box, or on this hook. I only had evidence when the decorations would change in the store. Plenty of my friends had been purchased even the orange purse and the green one too. Red purses went like wild fire because of the Christmas season. I guess purses were a popular item for presents. Oddly enough no one wanted me. Everyone was off to find their permanent homes, except me. Talk about being depressed.

As I stated before, my plight became worse. A sign hung in front of my section which read, "CLEARANCE." I was shocked! This was a fate worse than being trashed, or rather that was what I thought at the time. Clearance meant that we were either sold at a ridiculously low price or we would have to go back to the manufacturer – to be cleared out. Go back to Indonesia! No way! I could not even imagine what would happen to me. I was so hoping that someone, anyone would buy me. I was desperate and grasping at straws. I started to panic and wanted desperately to be anywhere but here. Have you ever seen a purse have an anxiety attack? It is not a pretty sight and can even be somewhat scary. Just when you think that a purse has moved suddenly, that is what we call anxiety.

If I had arms and legs, I would have jumped off this hook, ran away from this store, and get as far as I could possibly go. Now, that would have been a sight to behold – a runaway purse.

Unknown to me at that time, there was a person scouting out the store to see what could be easily shoplifted. In Walmart, even with security cameras, shoplifters were a problem. Constantly, there were police officers as well as store personnel on the prowl. However, there had been a few thieves who walked away with the goods.

This was the time which I encountered HER. I did not know her name until later. All I know was that I was snatched from the display rack which I had called home for six months. She literally ripped the sales tag off of me. Now, that hurt! She then proceeded to not only cram that into the pockets of her coat but also the protective packing that was inside of me to keep me fresh.

This industrious sixteen year old then ever so cautiously strolled through the store and approached the jewelry department. When no one was looking, she snatched five pairs of earrings, four bracelets, and a couple of watches. I knew this because she threw them inside of me and zipped me closed. She then wandered over to the electronics section, located in the back of the store. Plunk! Plunk! Plunk! Next came three phones and a couple of video games. How did she manage to get these was beyond my understanding. Just when I thought she was done, one more item came inside of me – a tube of lipstick. Interesting.

She then proceeded to make her way through the store taking her time as if she had been there all day with her yellow purse. Moments later, she had made her way to the front of the store. So far, so good. No one suspected, not the security officers, not personnel, not even other shoppers. She had it made. So simple it was, walking out the front door and then into the parking lot. I felt just a free as she did. I was at last out of that store and beginning yet another adventure with this nice young person. All of a sudden, this young shoplifter began to walk fast then take off into a run as if she were running for her life. Maybe she was.

# CHAPTER FOUR
# *THE RUNAWAY*

Serena had been on her own for about a year. She had endured as much as she could take for a teenager. Unfortunately, Serena had not known what it was like to have loving parents. She was born to an alcoholic father and drug addictive mother. Luckily, Serena had been born healthy.

Her parents decided to attend a rehabilitation facility during the time Serena's mother was pregnant just so her parents could keep her. Anything to keep Child Protective Services from taking Serena. But after she was born, that was a whole new ballgame, so to speak. They both went back to their old habits. Ten years later, Serena was put into foster care because her parents kept taking turns abusing her both physically and emotionally. I was amazed that it took that long for CPS to finally catch up to them.

After three years in foster care and floating from one house to another, the courts awarded custody of Serena back to her parents. They had both gone back to rehab only this time they both stayed clean. They both got jobs and actually kept them. She thought all was good with the world. Her relationship with her parents improved 180%. However, this was not to continue as her world abruptly came to an end.

Her father, who was in construction, met with an unfortunate accident which left her mother a widow and Serena, fatherless.

For a solid year, both Serena and her mother mourned her father's death. Then as if out of the blue, her mother began dating again. Serena was fourteen at this time. She had wished and wished that her mother would not be associated with the losers who she brought home time after time. By this time, Serena was growing into a beautiful young lady. Even her mother's so-called boyfriends began to notice.

It was her fifteenth birthday party, and Serena was celebrating it with her friends from school. All was good, except for the fact that her mother also had her boyfriend of the day at the party. But Serena just ignored him and continued to have fun with her friends. There was so much laughing, eating cake, and opening presents. Yes, she thought this was perhaps the best day of her life, literally. Even after everyone left, Serena was still on a happiness high. Nothing could possibly ruin that day, or so she thought.

Her mother and the boyfriend had been drinking, a lot. Serena was glad that her friends did not witness the so-called drunkenness. Her mother finally passed out on her bed. However, the boyfriend was still stumbling around speaking incoherently. He made his way to Serena's room. Whether he thought that was the mother's room or not, he just walked in to where Serena was fast asleep and dreaming of her party.

To begin with the boyfriend was not all that handsome, at least in Serena's eyes. She thought that he was fat and always smelling like a brewery. She was completely disgusted by the sight of him. She thought that her mother deserved better. But Serena's opinion was not warranted. Anyway, he slowly and quietly entered into

Serena's room. He discovered that he was not looking at the mother but Serena. What an opportunity, he thought! He gently put one hand over Serena's mouth and proceeded to slide into the bed next to her. He told her that if she uttered one word, just one, he would snuff the life out of her.

The next morning, Serena told her mother what had happened. She was called a liar and didn't know what she was talking about. She was also accused of being jealous of her own mother. Serena, feeling the hurt as if stabbed in the heart, just went back to her room crying the whole time. She almost wished that she was still back in foster care. This was when she began her plan to escape once and for all.

That night Serena packed up her duffle bag, took all the money she had hidden away, and grabbed her favorite stuffed animal for companionship. She even left a note to her mother telling her not to look for her, ever. Serena told her that her life is better with strangers than to be with a mother who would take the word of a loser boyfriend over her own daughter. Then she signed it with a goodbye, quietly walked through the front door, and never looked back.

Serena used some of her money to buy a bus ticket. She wanted to go where no one knew her, so she closed her eyes and just pointed to a destination. She was headed to Dallas, Texas. In Houston, where she was from, people would recognize her. At least in Dallas, she would have animosity.

So now to bring you up to date, Serena had been on her own for approximately one year either living on the streets or sleeping in parks. There was a time or two when she would find herself in the company of other wayward teens, but all they wanted to do is to get high on the drug of the day. That scene was not for her.

She shoplifted here and there, sell the items that she stole, and every once in a while stay in a motel just so she could take a shower and sleep in a real bed. It was one of those days when she found me in that Walmart store in Dallas. After she had pawned the stuff she stole that day, she still hung on to me as if I was a life saver. Maybe I was.

She kept all her money inside of me for she did not feel it would be safe anywhere else. For all purposes, she was happy, and I was content, in fact happy as well. At least I felt useful, and it felt good to bring happiness to someone.

One day that happiness came to an end or at least we both thought so. Serena was walking through downtown Dallas on weekend where the food trucks and local artists liked to converge. It was so busy and congested with people, but Serena held me close. She knew about purse snatchers. They were everywhere especially where there were lots of people. She knew who they were as well, except for one.

He came from out of nowhere. Serena had been looking at some artwork and immersed in a conversation with the artist when what seemed like a tornado on a skateboard swished by. One minute she had her purse (me), and the next it was gone. He had not only taken me but all of Serena's money – all she had.

# CHAPTER FIVE
# *THE PURSE SNATCHER*

In a blink of an eye, I left the company of sweet Serena and immediately became the property of one young man known on the streets and Scratch. He had been on the streets since he was fifteen. How was he to know that Serena was in the same boat? If he had, he would have left her alone. All Scratch knew was that he saw a nice-looking girl with a nice-looking purse (that's me) which probably had nice-looking money in it.

Clad only in a T-shirt and ragged blue jeans, Scratch pulled the purse under his arm as if he was holding a football. He ran like the wind towards the area where he lived. He could have passed for a running back of a football team or even a track star. In any case, this boy could run!

We finally reached our destination. It was a vacant apartment building with boarded up windows and a fence around the property to keep trespassers out. But it did not keep Scratch and his friends away. He made his way through an opening in the fence and pushed aside a board which covered a window to gain access inside the apartment of which he lived.

Once inside, he put me on a makeshift table and proceeded to dump out the contents that were inside of me. He pushed aside the tube of lipstick that Serena kept inside plus some other objects.

Scratch's complete attention was on the money. He thought that he hit the jackpot!

He counted out five $20s, three $10s, five $5s, four $1s, and some change. Wow! Not a bad haul! It was over 170 bucks including the change. Little did Scratch know that this was all the money in the world that Serena had. Gee, I hope that she would be OK.

Scratch came by his name about five years earlier than this event when he himself was only fifteen. His home life was somewhat similar to Serena's. It was dysfunctional anyway. His home had been a loving home at one time until a tragedy hit this happy family. His older brother had been killed while serving his country overseas when Scratch (aka James) had been thirteen. After this happened, it seemed that James just could not live up the expectations that his father had put on him. His mother was still forever grieving, and he was constantly being compared to his older brother. Doctors had put James's mom on anti-depressants, but so far they had not done any good. All he got from his mom is constant sobbing. To her he seemed invisible.

His father, on the other hand, was completely opposite. He ruled his house with a firm hand. Even though James was a good kid, he just wasn't good enough. For two years, all he heard from his father was, "Why can't you be more like your brother? You are always messing up." James was not a star athlete nor was he a straight 'A' student. No matter how hard he tried, James could not measure up to what his brother had accomplished. So one day, he had had enough. Soon after his fifteenth birthday, he took off. He did not even leave a note. Nothing, nada, zilch. He packed a few things,

## The Traveling Yellow Purse

simply climbed out his bedroom window, and took off into the night, just like Serena did.

Also like Serena, James wanted to get to a place where no one knew him. He resided in Austin, Texas. He began his journey by hitch hiking as far north as he could possibly go. That destination ended up being Dallas, Texas.

At first, he just hung out at the bus station in downtown Dallas where quite of few homeless people were known to frequent. After a couple of days, this activity began to spook him just a little. On the third day, he just started walking. He kept walking for what seemed about two hours when a bunch of kids just like him approached James. They first just kind of pushed him around until he told them why he was walking and that he was a runaway. A couple of the boys put their arms around him, told him their names, and hustled him off to this abandoned apartment building, the very same one in which he had continued to reside.

For five years, James would either shoplift or snatch purses just to survive. He was basically scratching by, thus his street name began, Scratch.

Scratch looked at me from one end to the other and decided that not only did he not want to keep this purse (me), but he could not even think of anyone who would want it either. Now, I was getting worried.

With his new found money, Scratch decided to go do a little shopping. On his way out of the apartment complex, he passed a large dumpster near a strip shopping area. In a flash, he tossed the purse (me) inside and closed the lid.

## Glenda Jensen

Oh wow! Now, I really have hit rock bottom. Look at me! Here I am surrounded by four dirty, stinky metal walls on top of dirty, stinky I don't know what. Oh no! Was that a rat?! No, it was more like five or six of those creatures scrambling around. I have never seen such a sight, and I believe they must be worse than roaches. Was this to be my fate, my final resting place? Geez! I hope not. I was beginning to think that maybe going back to Indonesia would at least have been better than this.

One day passed, then two. At last on the third day, my prayers had been answered. The lid of the dumpster slowly swung open. What seemed to be a friendly yet homely face peered inside. Her clothes were a bit ragged in appearance, but she smiled when she saw me. As her hands reached in to grab me, they shook slightly. By her appearance, her age looked to be about sixty, but I could be wrong. Quite often living on the streets can age a person beyond their years.

After this person rescued me from the rubble in which I laid, she dusted me off (that felt good) and smiled even bigger. Again I was to experience yet another adventure.

# CHAPTER SIX
# *HOMELESS HANNAH*

Hannah was not really homeless, but she might as well have been. She lived in a low-income housing apartment along with her cat, Manfred. Yes, she had a roof over her head and food in her refrigerator, but old habits were hard to give up.

Hannah had been homeless for 20 years until a good Samaritan took her under his wing. He got her into an adult shelter where they helped her to clean up then proceeded to get her on Medicaid and food stamps. She didn't begin her life on the streets, but she might had been better off. The story which floated around among the other homeless residents was that she was first thrown out of her parents' house upon graduation just because she was pretty. Good grief! Then to top it off her no-good ex-husband tossed her out as well. With no real education and no money, Hannah took to the streets. She barely survived from one day to the next. She basically became what was known as a dumpster diver.

Hannah knew the spots where halfway decent clothes were thrown out and left over food from grocery stores were dumped. Man, she had it made, or so she thought for about 20 years. The year Hannah turned fifty was when she noticed her age began to catch up with her body. Dumpster diving was not as easy as it was when she was younger. Even living in a cardboard box or in a shelter from time to time was not what it was cracked up to be either. So when this kind young man offered to help her, she did not say NO.

She had been in a shelter before so the protocols and rules were no different than the rest of them. Before this day, she had only stayed in one when the weather was bad outside. Now, she was willing to accept whatever help was offered. Even though Hannah had been living in her one-bedroom apartment, she would still cruise the neighborhood for anything worth diving for. This was when she found a special yellow purse (me).

After she had taken me home, Hannah washed me with gentle soap and carefully wiped me off with a wet rag. I felt like brand new again! I was perfectly happy being with Hannah. After all, she did take good care of me. She would take me on walks and proudly show me off to her street friends. But my thoughts kept going back to that sweet sixteen year old girl who saved me from the possibility of returning to Indonesia. Yes, my friends, I missed Serena. I wondered what she had been doing. Had she gotten off the streets? I hand no way of knowing at this point.

I had been with Hannah now going on two years. At least this was better than being on a hook in Walmart or worse being in a dumpster with a horrible future of ending up in some land fill. Yes, I was content. Not really gloriously happy but pleasingly content. So, I decided to accept what my fate was and give up ever seeing Serena again.

As days passed into weeks and weeks into months, there was a time when Hannah needed extra cash and fast. You see, Manfred, her cat had a lump under his chin, and he needed surgery to remove it. Unfortunately, Medicaid does not cover pets, and Hannah had no unearthly idea where the money was going to come from. She began to mentally take inventory of the items in her apartment of which she could sell. One of her items just so happened to be her special yellow purse (that's me).

Manfred was her friend, her family. So, if it was surgery he needed, then it was surgery he got. Hannah was not about to allow him to suffer in anyway.

With her grocery cart in tow along with the items she chose to sell, she proceeded to walk down the street pass the dumpsters, pass her favorite convenience store, and go right up to the thrift store of which she frequented quite so often. She had known everyone there from the time it opened several years ago up to present day.

As Hannah approached the thrift store, she again did a mental inventory of her things to sell: the TV she was given (she never watched it anyway), some books which she acquired through the years, a pair of roller skates which she recovered from a dumpster, a family broach which was given to her by her grandmother, some clothes, and her special yellow purse (me). Hannah entered Family Thrift Store with great confidence and expectations. She then immediately asked to speak with the manager, Roger Smart. As the manager walked from his office to the front of the store, he immediately recognized Hannah. He had done business with her before plus she had helped him during a dark emotional time in his life. Roger had lost his wife ten years ago to cancer, and he had turned to alcohol in order to numb the pain. Hannah came along just when he needed a friend and someone to listen. She not only helped him to get sober but helped him to find a job. He began as a sales clerk in this thrift store and then slowly moved up the ranks to manager.

Hannah was greeted with such enthusiasm that she almost forgot why she was there. When she saw Roger, a smile came over her face as she rolled her cat towards him. When they met in the middle of the store, hugs were exchanged along with tearful hellos. Hannah explained to him her circumstances, and he escorted her back to his office. She told him that she needed $200 for Manfred's surgery. He looked at the items that she brought and smiled as he gave her the cash. Not only did Hannah receive the $200, she also received an extra $200. Yes, today was a good day indeed.

As Hannah waved good bye, I couldn't help but think what my next adventure here in this store would be like. I may not be at Walmart, but at least it wasn't a dumpster either.

# CHAPTER SEVEN

## *THRIFT STORE SAGA*

Roger, the manager of Family Thrift Store, sought out an employee by the name of Samuel, Sam for short, to begin putting the items that Hannah brought in for display. He wasn't sure if anyone would buy the TV as it was a small one, and everyone wanted the big flat screens nowadays. But who knows? Maybe someone out there in the consumer world would want it. Sam put the TV with the other electronics then the broach was placed with the other jewelry. Now that piece might just bring a nice profit. Next the clothes were priced and hung up. When Roger had looked at those clothes, they looked familiar to him. He thought that he had sold those exact same items to Hannah. Finally, came the purse (me).

Instead of a hook, I was put on a shelf. I felt the presence of other purses. Some had been there for quite some time. I certainly hoped that was not going to be my fate. At least I would not be going back to Indonesia or be tossed into a dumpster. But still I did not want to be stuck on this shelf forever either. There were mostly brown, black, and white purses. Nothing stood out quite as much as I did. I began to feel rather special again. Gee! I wonder what Serena was doing. I really liked her. Maybe she'll come in the store and buy me, that is, if she has any money. All I knew was that I really did miss her. But time will tell; time will tell.

As the days passed, I began to become accustomed to the thrift store. The store was quite smaller than Walmart, so it gave off an aura of a down home feeling similar to feeling all fuzzy inside. But, of course, my insides weren't fuzzy but satiny. Anyway, it projected a good feeling. The employees were nice not just to customers but also to each other. Roger, the manager, was always giving complements. We were all just one big happy family.

The weekends were the busiest, as to be expected. Customers would come and go by the dozens it seemed. With each one coming through the door, I kept hoping that someone would buy me and take me home. Plus still no Serena. This adventure projected a bitter-sweet feeling or rather a sweet but sad feeling. By this time in my purse life, I began to give up the idea of ever seeing Serena again. But at least I thought about her. Even if no one did purchase me, I could see myself being happy in The Family Thrift Store with Roger, Sam, the other employees, and my fellow purses as constant companions. Yes, my friends, once again life was good.

Six months had passed and still no one had bought me. Yet, there were new purses added: a red one, another black one (as if there wasn't enough already), a pink one, and a blue one. On the other hand (if I had hands), two of my companion purses had been bought, both black. I guess black for accessories was a popular color. Why doesn't anyone like yellow? Yellow is a happy color, a bright color. I just don't understand it. Hmmmm. I will have to ponder this thought. As I have mentioned earlier in my story, I do ponder things quite a bit.

## The Traveling Yellow Purse

When the six months had come and gone, Spring was finally upon us. For some reason I felt super happy as if something wonderful was about to happen. The clock struck noon on a Wednesday when a kind-looking elderly lady walked into the store. She was accompanied by a younger woman who looked to be in her 50s along with another much younger woman to be about 20ish or maybe a little older. They walked around the store looking at clothes, books, and well just about everything. When they stopped by the purses, I felt a rush of anxiety. If I could have had the capability to yell out, I would have done just that. But all I could do is think loudly, "pick me, pick me!" Then just at that particular point in time, the elderly lady walked right up to me and picked me up. She held me up high, hung me on her arm, and looked inside. She then turned to her daughter and remarked, "Delores, this purse will match my new Easter dress perfectly." Her daughter smiled and replied, "Ok, mom. We'll get the purse and then we'll go get some lunch." When the three women approached the checkout counter, a familiar face was surprised and pleased all at the same time.

Roger could not help but reminisce about his boyhood days. "Lady Gretchen? Just how are you? I haven't seen you since I was a boy." The elderly woman, now known as Lady Gretchen turned to him and asked, "Do I know you, son?" Roger chuckled and said, "probably not. The last time you saw me I was only ten years old. Your husband, Coach Bob, was my little league baseball coach. I'm Roger Danfield. Remember? You used to bring us snacks after practice." Lady Gretchen, not really royalty but everyone called her that because of her kind and gentle characteristics, looked at Roger then reached out to give him a big hug.

Gretchen turned to her daughter with a smile on her face as big as the outdoors, "Delores, this is little Roger, the boy you used to play with a long time ago before we moved. Remember?" "Of course, mom. Now that you mention it, I do remember Roger." Delores then turned to Roger and said politely, "Roger, how are you? Yes, it has been a long time, hasn't it? So good to see you again. By the way, I'd like you to meet my daughter, Jennifer." They both shook hands upon greeting. "Maybe the next time I'm in the area, we can get caught up with what's been going on with our lives." Roger replied eagerly, "Delores, that would be great. I will look forward to seeing you again." With that being said, we were out the door and off to a restaurant to get some lunch, well at least they were. Me? I was off to yet another adventure.

# CHAPTER EIGHT

# *LADY GRETCHEN*

After lunch I was whisked away to yet another household. Only this time my new home was settled in a quaint suburban neighborhood of Dallas, Texas. No dumpsters, no boarded up windows, and no shelters either. The neighborhood had loads and loads of trees with the greenest lawns that I have ever seen. What a difference!

When I was carried into Lady Gretchen's home, I was awestruck. I have never ever seen a home so beautiful. This was heaven compared to where I had been before. I thought finally I had hit the jackpot. But through this entire splendor, I still was thinking about Serena. After all she was the one who initially rescued me, and for that I will be forever thankful.

Lady Gretchen was not born into a life of luxury. She and her husband worked hard for what she now enjoys. Her journey began during World War II when she resided in Sweden as a young girl in her teens. Her husband, Robert, had been an American soldier. They met while he was recuperating in a hospital in Sweden. Soon they fell in love and got married. Robert was granted a medical discharge with full benefits. He was even awarded a purple heart (soldiers received these for being wounded in battle).

Arriving in America began as a scary yet exciting adventure for young Gretchen. She had always wanted to travel there, but the opportunity never presented itself. Now here she was. Gretchen had taken a deep breath just to take it all in. "Wow," she thought, "America is ten times larger than Sweden, maybe more." When Gretchen and her new husband arrived in Dallas, Texas, Robert immediately started back to work. He held down a job prior to the war at General Motors located in Arlington, Texas, not too far from Dallas. His boss had explained that he would still have his job upon his return. Sure enough true to his word, Robert's boss welcomed him back with open arms.

In the meantime, Gretchen settled in their two bedroom apartment. She started to put a woman's touch to the place and boy did it need it. So while Robert was working, she would find herself cleaning, adding curtains, and re-arranging furniture. She also made sure that Robert would have a nice cooked meal every day when he came home from work. Many memories were made in this tiny apartment. However, they did not live there for long. Gretchen soon found herself to be pregnant. A third member was to be added to her family. When she found out, Gretchen just could not wait long enough for Robert to get home from work. She was so excited. She wanted everything to be perfect. She made sure that the apartment was spotless with a very special dinner cooking on the tiny stove. A linen tablecloth adorned their two chair kitchen table with flowers in the middle. Everything seemed to be going her way. She even had their radio tuned in to some of their favorite music.

As it approached the time for when Robert would be coming home, Gretchen made sure that she looked like a model out of a magazine. He would be pleasantly surprised and probably wondering what was going on. Finally, the door opened, and Robert walked in. Tired as usual, he plopped down into his favorite chair. All he needed was just a few minutes to relax and listen to some music. Music? He didn't recall at any time when he came home and music was playing. Oh well, he didn't mind. It sounded so soothing. He couldn't help but smell the delicious aroma coming from the kitchen. Did he forget their anniversary or a birthday? No, that wasn't it. So he got up from his chair and moseyed into the kitchen. He walked up to Gretchen while she was cooking and gently kissed her on the back of her neck. "Hey, gorgeous, what's going on? What's the special occasion?" Gretchen just could not contain herself. She turned around, gave Robert a hug, and said, "Nothing much, DADDY." He looked at her questionably and hollered, "a baby!" "We're having a baby!" He grabbed her and kissed her all over again. He couldn't wait to tell his parents and his coworkers at work. He felt like he was on cloud nine. So did Gretchen. Now she had to tell Robert that they had to move into a house.

Nine months later, a daughter was born. They named her Delores, after Robert's grandmother who passed the prior year. The family now lived in a nice two bedroom house. Somewhat bigger than the apartment, at least there was a yard for little Delores. They also added a dog, named Charlie so there would be another male in the family. Gretchen would often find herself chuckling at this reason to which Robert gave for getting the Golden Labrador. Charlie would grow up with Delores being her constant companion and body guard. He was just so protective of her.

Three years later, Gretchen found herself to be pregnant again. This time it was to be a boy. Boy howdy, was Robert happy. At last, someone to carry his name and someone to play catch with. Of course, he loved little Delores with all his heart. After all she was his little princess. But a son! That was different. However, this happiness came to a complete halt. Little Jonathan was born a sick little boy. By the time he was a year old, he had contracted pneumonia and never recovered from it. It broke both the hearts of Robert and Gretchen to bury their small baby boy. Robert just wasn't the same again after that. It seemed that the light in his eyes had flickered out. Another blow came to them as well. Gretchen could no longer have any more children. Thus Delores was to grow up without any siblings, but she made friends easily around the neighborhood including Roger Danfield.

By the time Delores had turned ten, the family moved once again. This time it was to a bigger house and a better neighborhood. After all Robert had been promoted and was making more money. He spent a lot of time at work. Maybe that's why he was promoted. Work seemed to be his outlet for coping with the loss of his son, his namesake. It was in this house where Robert retired, where Gretchen would be planning Delores's wedding, baking cookies for her grandchildren, and yes planning Robert's funeral.

Now here she was with her brand new yellow purse, that's me. At Easter, Gretchen proudly carried her new purse, which matched her new Easter dress, to church. She really could not wait to show it off. Delores and her family just would go along for the ride, so to speak, not saying a word. If this purse made Gretchen happy, then that was OK with them.

Two years had passed, and I was still hanging around at Gretchen's house. She had gotten rid of two or three of her other purses, but she hung on to me. Why? I don't know. Maybe there was a bonding between us. Who knows? It was also during this time that I had noticed that Gretchen rarely left her house. In fact, someone who looked like a nurse would come over from time to time. There was also someone who came over every afternoon to help around the house and help Gretchen when she needed it, like getting dressed, going to the bathroom, or even walking from one room to another. Gretchen was also hard-headed and strong-willed. She had constantly told Delores that she would not be caught dead in one of those nursing homes. She had heard some bad stories about them. That when someone goes in, they don't come out, alive that is. So they compromised on having someone come to Gretchen's house instead to help her out.

A year later, Gretchen was rushed to the hospital due to complications of the flu. It had gone into pneumonia. This kind lady was scared that she would not make it. After all she had just celebrated her 80th birthday. Maybe it was time to meet her maker and join Robert and dear Jonathan. As Delores sat at her bed side in the hospital, Gretchen whispered to her about her will and some other important papers in her desk drawer at the house. Delores promised her mother that she would read them. Three days later, dear Gretchen left this world to join her husband and son. Delores was left to make all of the funeral arrangements. This was a sad day for her. But at least, Delores had her own two sons to lean on. One of the provisions in the will was that whatever the family did not want and could not be sold in an Estate sale was to be donated to the homeless or to her favorite thrift store. So after the funeral, Delores and her sons found themselves going through Gretchen's things. This was hard because it seemed that everything would be bringing back memories of some sort. Finally, after everything was sorted through including pictures and other memorabilia, Delores decided to hire Estate sellers to handle the sale. She just could not bring herself to handle it. She also contacted a realtor to handle the sale of the house. This is how Johnson & Johnson Estate Sellers would step into the picture and handle the estate sale of Gretchen's things.

# CHAPTER NINE
## *THE ESTATE SALE*

This was a sad day indeed, because I knew that I was to welcome yet another adventure. Sheesh! Just so you know that I was getting kind of tired of all these adventures. I wish that I could find a permanent place. This thought took me back to Serena again. Golly, I sure miss her. I wish that she would just prance into this Estate sale and whisk me away.

The workers had arrived and began moving things around after Delores and her children had sorted through everything. Of course, I wasn't chosen. Not surprising. Anyway the hustle and bustle continued all day and even throughout the night. There were tables with all kinds of stuff arranged. In other words, someone with OCD (Obsessive Compulsive Disorder) would be proud. A table on the left showed nothing but purses, and the one on the right sported shoes. So naturally, finding me on the table on the left was evident. The other tables had piles of shirts, skirts, and dresses. There were also kitchen supplies such as pots, pans, and other kitchen miscellaneous. However, one table of items remained unclaimed which surprised me especially when no one in the family claimed these items. They were mementos and of some worth. Gosh, I was really taken aback when I saw a broach of which I had seen before. Now where had I seen that?

The broach which was gold in color and had been decorated with different colored flowers....lilies, I believe. I know! I remember seeing it at the thrift store where I was purchased by Ms. Gretchen. We rode home together in the plastic bag provided upon any sale. Imagine that! I had forgotten all about that, as if a purse could have a memory. But you just never know about me. Hehehehehe. Anyway I wanted to shout or at least wave at my buddy, the broach. After all, if you share a bag, you have bonded. Think about it. Any who, purses can't shout nor wave. Darn it! But we can think, dream, and wish.

Finally, the Estate Sale opened for business. Women flocked to the clothes mostly, and the men darted to the display of manly man tools. A lot of jabber could be heard throughout the sale. No words could be legible. After all, when a bunch of people get together under one roof and begin talking, it becomes noise. No one could be heard, and really no one cared what the others were talking about. But I cared!! I wanted to know where I was going to next! Wouldn't it be cool if Serena showed up?

Table by table objects were disappearing. It seemed to me that not one woman wanted a yellow purse, not even a teenager or young girl. Gosh! I felt neglected. On my table of purses, many purses of different colors stood out like circus clowns. A red one was chosen by a woman who already sported red shoes. Guess she wanted to match. Who knows? Not me! The next purse chosen was a green one. Really? Green? However, a young girl looked at it and just swooned. She thought it was the cutest thing since dollar

## The Traveling Yellow Purse

bills. Oh well, to each their own! Purses left besides me that could be displayed were a purple one, a brown one, a black one, and a white one. Which one will disappear next? Hmmmm, interesting situation.

The next person to meander over to the purse display proved to be a man. Wait a minute! A man! Really? What would a man want with a purse? Maybe he was shopping for his wife or girlfriend. Hmmmmm, another interesting situation. So he circled the table a couple of times, and I kept thinking, "pick me! I don't care!" But he then whistled and hollered at some woman across the room. She quickly made her way to the purse table with haste. In my mind I had all my threads crossed just hoping that she would choose me. If I had eyes, I would be closing them and saying a prayer. Then all of a sudden, she yelped loudly, "thank you Lord; I found it! The perfect purple purse to match my new outfit!" She then turned to her husband/boyfriend and planted a big kiss on his cheek. They both walked away happier than a pair of rabbits on a honeymoon. I was still wondering of Serena would ever show up. Gosh I miss her. After all, she was the first person that I came in contact with. In my mind, we just bonded like peanut butter and jelly. The black purse was the next to disappear then the brown one. All that was left on the purse table was the white one and me. Ho Hum! The hour of the end of the estate sale was soon approaching. It was a race to see which one of us would be the one to leave the table. At that point, an elderly lady slowly walked over to the purse table and gently picked up the white purse. The smile on her face lit up the whole room. So, here I am the only one left and no one to get me. All of a sudden just before the door closed, a young girl showed up huffing and puffing. SERENA!!

# CHAPTER TEN
# *THE FINAL DESTINATION*

"SERENA! SERENA! SERENA! I'm over here at the purse table!" Gosh I wish that she could hear me. She's over by the rack of dresses. Dresses in my opinion are just so prissy. It's almost like they think they're cute or something. Just so stuck up! However, women and girls love to swish them around on the rack and end up buying several. Go figure! So now she's looking at pots and pans. Hmmmmm! I wonder what's up? When I knew her, Serena proved to be homeless by the way she was dressed and where she lived – the streets. If my memory serves me right, we met in a Walmart, and she stole me right under their eyes. But the times we had were unforgettable. Now I'm cheering in silence that she would make her way over to where I am. Maybe she'll see the shoes! Come on, Serena! Look this way, please.

Now she's looking at sheets and blankets. Maybe she isn't homeless anymore. Maybe? That would be so cool! We could have our own place! We would be together again! Yeah! Oh wait! Here she comes! Come on, Serena. Just go a few steps to your left, and you'll be here. She's looking around the room as if looking for something specific. So far, she hasn't bought anything. Hmmmmm! She's at the shoe table now. Wait for it! Wait for it! She sees me! Yes, yes, yes! If I could jump, I would. She picks me up just smiling so big that the heavens should be shining. At last we will be together again.

Serena calmly walks up to the person taking money and hands over whatever I'm worth. We're walking out the door, and I can feel the sunshine barreling down on me. Dang! It feels good! If I could smile, that's what I would be doing. Now, I wonder where we are going. Serena continues to walk down the street away from the Estate sale. Further and further we go and then we walk to a parking lot where there are different stores there. We walk right into a store which sports dresses. Again go figure! But as long as Serena is happy, then I'm happy. She anxiously shows me off to her coworkers. Yes, I say coworkers because Serena has a job working in this so called dress shop. Could that mean she's no longer homeless? The mystery continues. She takes me to the back of the store and proceeds to put her stuff out of the purse which she is using into me. I feel the love. Yes, this yellow purse is loved by the only human whom I can love back.

As the day continues, only a few customers come in to look at the dresses. Did I say they are prissy? My opinion! Some dresses left the premises. Yeah! I say, "have a good life, dresses." When the last customer left, the boss lady began to close up shop by turning off the lights and then locking doors. Serena walks out the front door with me in tow. Wait a minute! What happened to the other purse? Hehehe! Who cares? So we walk a couple of blocks just to stop at a thing on four wheels. I believe it is called an automobile, car for short. Serena reaches inside of me and pulls out what looks like a key. She slowly unlocks this so called car. Hold on! Serena has a car? Awesome! We back up and proceed to go for what seems about 30 minutes. I have no unearthly idea where we are going. We pass a building which sports a billboard that advertises a shelter for homeless teenagers. Serena remembers when she lived there and how the people there aided her in getting her life back together and even help in finding a job. Wow! A lot has happened since I last saw her.

We then come to a stop which translates to PARK in car language. She comes around to where I'm at and gently gets me out of the car and makes sure it's locked. She faces a large building, and no, it's not a house. However, it is an apartment building, I believe that is what it's called. It's three stories, but Serena lives on the second story. Wow! Serena has her own place? So cool! We walk up two flights of stairs to get to her apartment. Again she pulls out another key and puts it into the lock on the door. As she opens the door, a guy is standing there. No it's not Scratch. I really did not like him. Well after all, he threw me in a dumpster. Gosh darn! It's someone else by the name of John. He gently pulls Serena close to him and kisses her. Oh my goodness! What's this all about? My questions are answered when he says, "what kind of day did my beautiful wife have?" Serena turns to him and says, "look, John, I found the Yellow purse. You know the one that I had stolen all those years ago? Well, here it is." With those words of love, I knew that all my adventures and travels are over. I will be happy for the rest of my Yellow purse life here with Serena.

# EPILOGUE

By now my readers or rather audience has figured out what happens to Serena. So, let's see what has happened to the rest of the characters.

1.  *The Purse Snatcher*

Scratch aka James discovers that he has family in another town, so he travels to live with them. They help him to clean up and yes get a job too. He becomes an assistant manager at a Walmart. Go figure!

2.  *Homeless Hannah*

Even though Ms. Hannah never really proves to be homeless, she appears to be that way. However, friends help her to find an apartment complex of which she could easily afford and live comfortably. By the way, her cat, Manfred, came out of his surgery like a champ and continues to live healthily.

3.  *Lady Gretchen*

No need to discuss what happens to Lady Gretchen. However, because of her unfortunate circumstance, Serena is reunited with her beloved Yellow purse.

## ALL'S WELL THAT ENDS WELL!!

## *About the Author*

***Glenda Lee Jensen*** is a retired English teacher who attributes her imaginative and creative writing to the many family stories that her grandparents told her while she was growing up. Not only family has inspired her to write but also her former students. She also gives some credibility to her own imagination while growing up whether it is playing cowboys and Indians with her neighbors using bicycles as horses or pretending to swing through the jungles on a swing set. Glenda is currently a freelance writer who also has had two poems and one novel published.

Glenda currently resides in Mesquite, Texas along with her dog, Ricky. She is the mother of three grown children and six grandchildren who also have been an inspiration for her writing.

www.ingramcontent.com/pod-product-compliance
Lightning Source LLC
LaVergne TN
LVHW020443080526
838202LV00055B/5321